P9-CAO-238

USBORNE FIRST READING
Level Three

WITHDRAWN

The Emperor and the Nightingale

Retold by Rosie Dickins

Illustrated by
Graham Philpot

Reading Consultant: Alison Kelly
Roehampton University

Hussey-Mayfield Memorial
Public Library
Zionsville, IN 46077

The Emperor of China was a very proud man. He always wanted the best of everything.

His palace was made of fine white bricks. The roof was solid gold.

The garden was full of bright flowers with silver bells. They tinkled in the wind.

The garden was very big. It was so big that even the Emperor never saw it all.

He never saw the little brown nightingale who lived in the trees.

But other people saw the nightingale.

The gardener saw her every day. He liked to listen to her singing.

Her songs always made him smile.

One day, the Emperor was reading a book about his wonderful palace.

The book said: "*The garden is full of bells that tinkle sweetly.*"

The Emperor smiled – but the next page made him frown. It went on: "*But the nightingale's song sounds sweeter than the bells!*"

"Why haven't I heard this nightingale?" snapped the Emperor. "Bring it to sing in the palace – now!"

The palace servants never went into the garden. They didn't know anything about the nightingale. But they didn't dare tell the Emperor.

They searched high and low. They looked under flowers...

and behind bushes.

In the end, they had to ask the gardener.

"I can show you the nightingale," he said.

They walked and walked. Suddenly, they heard a croak.

"The nightingale!" cried the servants.

The gardener smiled. "No, that's a frog in the pond," he replied.

A little later, they heard a loud MOO.

"The nightingale!" shouted the servants.

"No, that's a cow in the field," the gardener told them. He was trying not to laugh.

In the end, they came to a tree. Just then, the nightingale began to sing.

When she finished, the servants clapped. "Little bird, the Emperor wants you to sing in his palace," they said.

"My songs sound best out here, among the trees," said the bird, "but I will come."

And she flew back to
the palace with them.

The Emperor was surprised to see such a little brown bird.

But when she sang, he was enchanted by her voice.

The Emperor liked her voice so much, he ordered her to stay and sing to him every day.

The Emperor gave the nightingale a silver cage. But she missed living outside, among the trees.

Soon, the little brown bird was famous. Even the Emperor of Japan came to hear her sing.

One day, a big box arrived at the palace.

Inside, there was another nightingale. This one had sparkling golden feathers. Its eyes were made of rubies.

When you turned a key, it sang like the little brown bird – well, sort of...

although the tune was always exactly the same.

The Emperor was very happy.

He was so happy, he forgot all about the little brown bird. She flew away – and nobody noticed.

The Emperor played the golden nightingale every morning...

and every evening.

Until one day,
instead of singing...

it went *whizz-whirr*
and *ker-plunk*.

Something had broken inside. No one knew how to fix it.

Now the Emperor longed for the little brown bird. But no one could find her – not even the gardener.

Then the Emperor became sick. He lay in bed, staring sadly at his broken bird.

His room was full of silence and shadows. The doctors said he was close to death.

Suddenly, the sound of birdsong filled the air. It was the real nightingale.

She had found out the Emperor was sick. So she had come back to sing for him.

She sang so sweetly that the shadows seemed to fade. The Emperor smiled – and he began to get better.

Soon, the Emperor was well again. "I'm sure the nightingale cured me," he thought.

"Please stay," he begged the little bird. "You can have a golden cage and all the servants you want!"

"I prefer to live outside among the trees," the nightingale replied. And she flew away.

The Emperor was very sad. He asked the gardener to plant a tree under his window.

"It will remind me of the nightingale," he said.

The gardener watered the tree every day. It grew and grew.

One day, the Emperor heard something flutter past his window. He looked out.

To his surprise, he saw *two* nightingales. They were building a nest in the tree.

And when they sang, everyone in the palace smiled to hear them – the Emperor most of all.

The story of the Emperor and the nightingale was first told by Hans Christian Andersen. He was born in Denmark in 1805, the son of a poor shoemaker. He left home at fourteen to seek his fortune and became famous all over the world as a writer of fairy tales.

Series editor: Lesley Sims

Designed by Louise Flutter

First published in 2007 by Usborne Publishing Ltd., Usborne House, 83-85 Saffron Hill, London EC1N 8RT, England. www.usborne.com
Copyright © 2007 Usborne Publishing Ltd.

All rights reserved. No part of this publication may be reproduced, stored in a retrieval system or transmitted in any form or by any means, electronic, mechanical, photocopying, recording or otherwise without the prior permission of the publisher. The name Usborne and the devices are Trade Marks of Usborne Publishing Ltd.
Printed in China. UE. First published in America in 2007.

05/09

USBORNE FIRST READING
Level Four

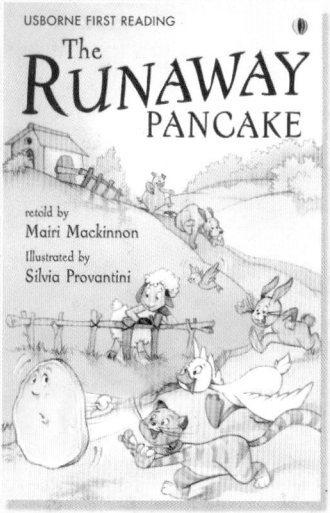

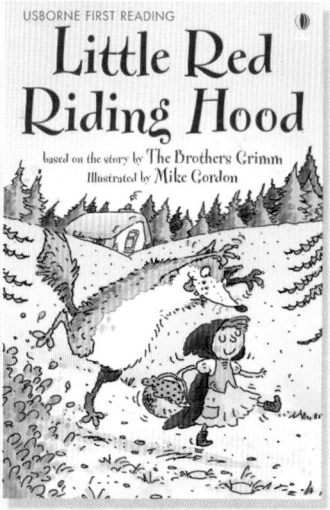